LIFE'S A BITCH

By

Rina Moriarty

ISBN 1-906027-06-4
ISBN 978-1-906027-06-3

Cover design by eprint Ltd.
Printed and bound in Ireland.

LIFE'S A BITCH

By

Rina Moriarty

CHAPTER 1

George was one of twelve children born into a large family in a small town in Wales in the 1950s. His father had worked in the coalmine and his father before him. In total, three past generations of Jones' had earned their crust in the coalmines. His father was a proud man who spoke very little and who was very strict with all of his children. He worked hard; that was the way it was meant to be, in his understanding.

His mother was a woman of few words, not unlike his father. Her life centred around her husband and children. Her life was about being a devoted wife and a good mother to her children. George had six sisters and five brothers. He seldom mixed or played with any of them. He was a loner who preferred his own company. He was happy helping his mother in the household - cleaning, cooking, ironing, washing and baking. His mother often remarked on how George was more helpful in the household than all of his sisters put together.

When George was nineteen years old, he decided to leave the family nest to spread his wings and start making a life of his own. He was mature enough to realise that, in such a large family, one less would lighten the burden of his parents. He went to London to look for work. The family agreed that George would stay with his Uncle Bob and Auntie Alice while he was job hunting. Soon, he got a job in a bakery in a small street on the outskirts of London. The hours were long. He started work at four a.m. each morning. It paid well and had an added bonus of a modest bed-sit directly over the bakery. Uncle Bob and Auntie Alice helped him to move in. He was happy at last. He was finally free to live his own life, which gave him a great sense of freedom. Life's brilliant, he would often think to himself.

George wrote home frequently to his mother and family in Wales. He couldn't wait to boast about his new job and the little bed-sit that was now his home. It was small but he put his own personal touches to it. He hung up family photographs and new curtains on the window that his mother had sown for him with precision and love. She also gave him an old family heirloom of a white lacy tablecloth that she thought would look so well when anyone came to visit George. Appearances were so important to her.

Across the street from the bakery was a small quaint corner shop that specialised in making homemade sweets of many different varieties. The creamy homemade chocolate truffles were, without a doubt, the most popular amongst the customers. It was a family run business owned by the Crosby's. Granny Crosby, Annie, now in her eighties but as sharp and as 'with it' as a woman half her age, carried in her head and also handwritten, stored in an old cigarette box, the family's secret chocolate recipe, passed down from generation to generation. Now it was Annie and her only granddaughter, Jenny, who continued the family art of sweet making. They worked well together and loved each other dearly.

Jenny's parents had died in a car crash when she was only five years old. Granny Annie provided Jenny with all the love, security and affection that equalled parenting of a mother and father. Jenny was a very shy girl but her grandmother always made her feel like she was the most important girl on the planet.

George had a weakness for the Crosby butter-rich chocolate truffles presented so well in a cream coloured box, tied up discreetly with a satin pink bow that made the chocolates even more pleasing to the eye. Every Friday, George would buy his weekly treat of truffles. Soon, Jenny and George started to chat and get to know each other.

As the weeks went by, George looked forward to Fridays. Granny Annie saw how Jenny smiled and blushed when George came into the shop. Sometimes Jenny's hand would accidentally touch against George's when she handed him over his chocolate truffles. Grandmother Annie would purposefully leave the shop, saying: 'I'm going to have a cup of tea in the back kitchen, my dear,' so that George and Jenny could be alone.

One Friday evening, George finally plucked up the courage to ask Jenny to accompany him to the local pictures the following Wednesday. The film, *Gone with the Wind*, was showing at the time. Jenny could feel her heart missing a beat with delight and couldn't wait to reply, 'yes, yes,' as George, almost sick with fear of being turned down, stumbled and stuttered over his words. 'Yes, yes,' Jenny replied and he felt relief and a sense of peace came over him. He had asked her out after all the weeks of hoping and his wish had finally been granted.

Wednesday night arrived. Jenny tried on four different dresses until, finally, Granny and Jenny agreed on the baby blue silk dress tied neatly at the waist with a pink bow that showed off her tiny waist. George wore his crisp, freshly starched white shirt, which his mother had given him as a birthday present. He combed his black hair five or six times and put on Brylcream to stop it from sticking up. Finally, he got it right, turned off the light and went to pick up Jenny. As they waited in the queue for the picture to start, he secretly admired her beautiful blue eyes and her perfectly formed features. This was the beginning of something wonderful, he thought and, for some reason, it was the first time in his life that he was with someone who made him feel that he could be himself.

Soon, the Wednesday night picture became a ritual with them both. Sunday became their day for taking the bus to the countryside where they would have a picnic and go walking in the woods.

Their feelings for each other became stronger and stronger. The bond that tied them was love of an emotional kind. Apart from holding hands, their relationship was not a physical one. Neither of them needed or desired a sexual relationship; at least not for now.

As the months rolled by, Jenny knew she wanted to get married and have a family. She found herself looking at wedding gowns in the window of a bridal shop close by and fantasised about wearing one of them. Irish lace, she thought to herself, I would love that.

Soon, her fantasy turned to reality when George asked her to marry him. When he asked Grandmother Annie for her blessing she cried tears of joy because she knew she might not have much longer to live and knowing that her granddaughter had met someone who loved her dearly and almost as much as she did gave her a sense of peace.

It was a small country wedding. Jenny looked very graceful and beautiful. Granny dipped into her savings from years of chocolate making for her granddaughter's special day. All the guests and friends of the Crosby's remarked on the beautiful couple who had met and fallen in love and wished them all the joy and happiness in the world.

A year to the day, 4 September, Jenny gave birth to a ten-pound baby girl. Sadly, on that very day, Granny Annie got a massive heart attack and died in another part of the same hospital. A beautiful old woman, who had given so much all her life, was finally called to her eternal rest and would be reunited with her past love, Nicholas.

Jenny felt cheated but, as time went by, her pain and hurt became easier to bear. The thought that her little girl, whom she had christened Annie Jennifer Jones, as well as being a gift from God, was also a part of Annie, gave her much consolation.

By the time young Annie had started school five years later, George and Jenny's marriage was in trouble. Jenny seemed to be devoting all her love and affection, time and energy to Annie. It seemed to him that she was distancing herself more and more from him. He tried to reassure himself that things would eventually get back to the way they were before Annie was born but Jenny just grew colder and colder towards him. Eventually, she asked him to move out of their bedroom.

Deep down, George was relieved because, although he had not wanted to admit it, not even to himself, he was no longer attracted to the woman he once loved. The truth was that sex had become repulsive to him.

George's childhood and adolescence had been haunted by feelings he could never share with anyone. All those old feelings came rushing back now, feelings that he had painted over, like new paint over old. George had always wished he had been born a girl. 'I wish I had been born a girl,' he cried out. There, I've said it, he remarked to himself. He got flashbacks of the times his mother's or sisters' dresses were thrown on the floor and he would try them on and the times he would wear their lipstick and high heels.

6

Over the years, he had tried to rationalise these episodes by saying that he was just a child and that he had grown out of it.

Now George's nightmare was back. One day when Jenny was out, he decided that he would have to do it; he would have to know, once and for all. He sneaked into her bedroom. He started by trying on her nylon hold-ups, progressing to her dress and then, finally, to her lipstick. He stared at himself in the mirror. He had the physical shape and body of a man but inside he felt like a woman with all the feelings of a woman. This wasn't the way things were supposed to be. Why, for God's sake, hadn't he been born a girl? Why couldn't he be normal, like everybody else? He felt so trapped.

As the tears streamed down his cheeks, his inner turmoil grew stronger and stronger until finally, he retched into the bedroom sink. With the physical release came the sudden acknowledgement: 'I am,' he shouted, 'a woman.' God help me, he thought, but this is who I really am.

George now knew that he was living a lie and that he could no longer keep up the pretence of his marriage. He would have to leave Jenny and Annie. There was no other way. He couldn't pretend any more, not to them, not to himself. He knew they were well looked after financially. At least that was one problem he would not have to deal with.

CHAPTER 2

George decided that he would have to have a sex change. He knew that it would not be easy and that it would involve physical, emotional and mental pain. He would have to be strong but it would be worth it because it was what he truly wanted. He also made the decision to start his new life as a woman in a new country. America, he thought, nobody would know him there. That is where he would go.

After researching the process thoroughly, he booked into a highly recommended clinic. He was very nervous because, after all, this was no ordinary medical matter. Before anything was done, he had to attend a meeting with the doctors who would carry out the surgery. They explained the medical procedures as well as the psychological impact. He would have to go for hormone treatment twelve months prior to the final operation. As time progressed on the hormone treatment, George's main features became less and less manly. His voice softened and he looked more like a woman. He received counselling over the months before the final operation. The pain he went through, both physically and emotionally, was excruciating.

At last it was all over. When he looked in the mirror back in his apartment, he was finally happy with what he had become. Tears of relief, sadness and hope, at last, tumbled down his face. 'Hope,' he declared, 'that is what I will call myself. Hope.'

In the following months, George, now Hope, despite all *her* positivity, was haunted by thoughts of her family at home in Wales and, most painful of all, her wife and child. The loneliness she felt was stifling. Eventually, she began to block out these memories so that she could get on with the rest of her life.

She found a job in a large library and this kept her busy. She began to make new friends. Emily and Grace, both in their early fifties, had worked in the library all their working lives. They now took Hope under their wing. They chatted about different books and best sellers and books they had not yet read. All three shared a love of poetry. Hope, Emily and Grace soon started to socialise together. They went to the ballet, opera and various social occasions. Hope realised that she was now, finally, accepted totally as a woman.

Hope started to pray a lot, something she had never done in the past. She found peace now when she prayed and went to Church. After all, she felt, God was the only one who knew her secret pain. She prayed for strength and for God's love to carry her through. Sometimes she felt very angry with God for dealing her this terrible heavy cross. She began visiting her local church on a daily basis. It became her haven of peace and tranquillity. Although she couldn't deny her loneliness, she did feel a sense of inner peace knowing that she was now a woman, that she had been true to herself and that her outer self now reflected the inner.

CHAPTER 3

Emily and Grace, now in their early sixties, were discussing their retirement.

'I am six months younger than you. You retire first and I will follow,' Grace teased Emily.

'Why don't we both retire now?' Emily asked. 'We could do the things we've always wanted to do.'

The two women owned their own separate houses. They decided to sell both houses and buy one they had seen for sale that overlooked the lake. It had a flower garden and there were roses growing around the doorway. There were also other houses nearby, something that reassured them both, in the event that they would ever need help. They were realistic about the fact that they were growing old.

Hope and the rest of the library staff organised a retirement party for Emily and Grace. Their boss, Mr. Roberts, shook their hands and presented them with two engraved gold watches and said such touching words in regards to the two outstanding workers who had spent a lifetime in the library. He spoke very highly of them. 'Without you both, it's the end of an era.'

Not a man to normally show emotion, his glasses had misted over. He took them off, saying: 'Oh, it's just some dust gone into my eye.' Still, some tears managed to trickle down and lodge in the page where he had written his warm speech for these two, very special ladies. 'Three cheers,' he shouted, 'for Emily and Grace.'

'Well, this had to happen at some time,' remarked Grace. 'Retirement at last!'

Hope felt so alone. She knew that she had to let Emily and Grace go and so she tried to be strong. After all, she thought, I love them dearly and I want them both to be happy. I shouldn't be thinking of myself. Hope tried to cover up her inner feelings with smiles and laughter. 'I will come to visit you,' she laughed, 'and when I do, I want you to roll out the red carpet for me.'

'Nothing less for you, Hope,' replied Emily.

'We are going to miss you. It's a pity you're not the same age, because if you were, we would not go anywhere without you, our dear, dear friend,' added Emily. The three huddled together and fought back the tears with artificial smiles.

Hope went home to her empty apartment that evening and for some reason, even though it was a warm, clammy evening, she felt colder and more alone than ever before. She suddenly felt the need to get out the old trunk buried under blankets and old clothes in her bedroom. This was her trunk of memories. She lifted out the family photograph album and sat down on the bed to look at the photographs. She came to one of old Granny Annie, Jenny and George. She remembered the day clearly. All three smiled like a sunbeam and the warmth of all their love radiated out to her. It hit her heart like a bolt of lightning. She felt total despair and emptiness. It was as if her life-light had finally been extinguished.

Rocking backwards and forwards, tears streaming down her cheeks, Hope cried out to God to help her. From the very depths of her being, she asked God to ease her pain and help her find some peace.

Tears spent, she continued looking through her photographs and there she was, Baby Annie Jennifer Jones. For ten years, Hope had never once found the courage to open the trunk. It contained all those memories that she wanted to try to forget. Now, having opened it, she couldn't help but feel that her heart was breaking into a million tiny pieces. 'Ten years. Annie Jennifer is almost fifteen years old,' she calculated. She wondered what her daughter looked like. She must surely be beautiful, just like her mother. All the memories Hope had tried to contain for all these years came bursting through like a river bursting through its banks.

Hope suddenly felt the need to write to Annie to let her know how she felt. She went over to her writing desk and sat down on the comfortable old chair. Without thinking, she started to write and it was as if the words just came flowing from her pen.

My Precious Daughter,

You didn't deserve a parent like me, even though I never stopped loving you, not for one second. Although I do not have the right to ask anything of you, my special daughter, my wish is that somewhere in you heart you could learn to forgive me for not being the kind of father you so richly deserve. Though our circumstances are very unusual and we are not like other families, I want you to know that my love for you could fill heaven and earth.

I wish you the wings to fly. I wish you the vision to dream wildly, the heart to love deeply and the spirit to embrace all the beauty in life.

Your Loving Father

Hope felt weak and exhausted. She slumped into the chair with the letter to her daughter clasped with both hands to her breast. She soon fell asleep. She awoke with a stiff neck and looked at the clock. It had just struck seven a.m. My God, I must have drifted off, she thought. Luckily, it was Sunday and she did not have to go to work. She needed to collect her thoughts and decide whether or not she would send Annie the letter. She was full of indecision. There was nothing in this world that Hope wanted more than to let her daughter know how much she loved her but she didn't know if it would be in Annie's best interests to hear from her father after so long – a father who was no longer a man.

She decided to put off making a decision until she had eaten breakfast. She proceeded into the kitchen where she scrambled some eggs and made coffee. When she had finished eating, she took the dishes over to the sink to do the washing up. She suddenly realised that she had been washing and drying the same dishes over and over again.

'It's time to put things right,' Hope kept saying aloud. For some time now she had been talking aloud as though she were speaking to someone who knew her deepest, darkest secrets. 'I can't send the letter directly to Annie, she's too young to understand the person I really am. Even I, as an adult, sometimes feel that my life and all that I have been through is just a nightmare from which I will soon awaken. First, I have to write to Jenny; after all, I walked away from her without leaving a note - no explanation, nothing. Then there's my family in Wales. I just couldn't handle their rejection, disgust and humiliation. I was, and still am, somebody they could never accept. I have to write to Jenny and try to explain, as best I can, the torment and pain that goes with being born different. All I want is to be accepted for the person I am without being judged or criticised but the world just doesn't accept difference, does it?'

Over the years, Hope had tried to reassure herself by saying that everybody in London and Wales would presume George was dead. Being dead, in Hope's mind, would have made things easier for all her loved ones. Now, though, she finally realised it was time to let go of all her fears and, after all the years of hiding, bring the secrets of the past to the surface. It was time for her family to finally hear the truth, despite the pain of revealing everything to them.

Hope sat down to write a letter to Jenny whom she had never wanted to hurt or cause so much pain. She wrote and re-wrote each line of her letter, tore out page after page until, eventually, she was happy with her words. She explained everything as best she could and asked for forgiveness. At last, the truth had unfolded, bringing Hope a sense of relief; the kind of relief one feels after leaving a confessional. Jenny was the only one who could give Hope her absolution.

She took out a large white envelope from the writing desk drawer. Although she had written two separate letters for Jenny and Annie, she put them both in this envelope and addressed it to Jenny. All she could do now was pray that Jenny would understand and find it in her heart to forgive her. It would be up to Jenny now to pass this letter on to her dear daughter and maybe try and explain this horrible, sad secret to her. If she felt that she wanted to protect Annie from this awful truth, Hope would understand. Both letters were now complete and ready for posting on Monday. It was strange, Hope realised; her life's past and future were in that ordinary white envelope.

CHAPTER 4

On a sunny April morning in London, Jenny was going through the usual busy daily routine. 'Hurry up Annie, get out of that bed! Get down here for your breakfast or you'll be late for school and I don't want any more complaints from teachers about you being late again. After all, Annie, this is an important school year for you with all those exams!'

'Be down in a flash, Mother,' shouted Annie, struggling to tie a perfect knot in her school tie. In the kitchen, she gulped down her bowl of porridge, her absolute favourite breakfast food, and drank her glass of freshly squeezed orange juice. 'Where is my lunch box, Mother?' she asked. Lunchbox in hand, 'I'd better dash,' she shouted, hurrying out the door for her seven-minute walk to school.

On her way to school, Annie tried counting the amount of footsteps it would take her to get there, but got distracted by a dog who growled at her because she was walking on his territory as he chewed on the bone his master had given him as a treat.

Jenny tidied the kitchen before looking in on her daughter's room. Oh my, she smiled to herself, teenagers!

Annie's clothes were strewn everywhere. Jenny knew she shouldn't be picking up after her all the time but Annie's idea of tidying was so different to her own! Ah, but she was a good girl all the same, always ready to help out in the shop as soon as she arrived in from school each day. Annie had developed an interest in the family trade of making and selling chocolate sweets. She had the same sense of pride in the littler corner shop that her mother had inherited from her grandmother. Jenny could never see herself wanting it any other way than running her own family business where she was her own boss.

Jenny was now in a relationship with John Ellis, whom she had known since childhood. They had gone to school together. He was now, himself, a teacher in the same school he attended as a child. So, in a way, John comforted Jenny and was there for her when George left her. Jenny and John had often talked about him moving in with Jenny and Annie but decided against it out of respect for Annie. After all, Jenny was still officially married to George. It was not an open and closed case. Nothing was ever definite about George. There were still a lot of unresolved issues as to his whereabouts. Was he dead? Did he run away because he was afraid to commit to her? Did he lose his memory? Had he met someone else? The list of possibilities was endless.

At first, George's parents and family would often talk to Jenny about George and his whereabouts but in the latter years they had spoken less and less of what might have happened to him. 'We all have to accept that George is dead and that he is not coming back,' they would say to her.

When Jenny and Annie visited them in Wales, Annie's grandparents would welcome them with open arms. They adored Annie and thought of Jenny as one of their own. George's parents felt that their son had let them down badly. They even accepted John Ellis into the family, much to the delight of Jenny. They saw that he was a rock for both Jenny and Annie. He was kind and caring and Annie had a very good relationship with him. She always went to him for help with maths and science, as these were the subjects he taught. In Annie's view, John was cool! He never got angry, no matter how many times she would ask him to explain a sum to her.

By eleven o'clock, Jenny felt she deserved a nice cup of tea and a lovely, sugary doughnut. The shop was quiet. It always was on a Monday.

'Good morning, Mrs. Jones, and how are you today?' Ben, the postman said as he handed Jenny her mail.

'Fine thanks, Ben. I'm just having my elevenses. There's one more doughnut in the box, you are more than welcome to join me,' remarked Jenny.

'Well, how could I refuse such a beautiful woman on a beautiful Monday morning!'

'Two sugars, isn't it, Ben, with a tint of milk?'

'Yes, where would I be without your pampering on this lovely morning? I'll have to cut down on the sugar, Jenny.

The wife thinks I'm getting too plump.' He rolled his hand over his belly and remarked, 'I'm starting to look like Santa Claus.'

'What harm?' smiled Jenny. 'You're pleasantly plump.'

'You're such a rogue, Jenny Jones!' replied Ben with a laugh. 'Now, I'll have to leave you and continue my deliveries to the twenty cottages near the old railway. No doubt, Jenny, but you make the finest tea and treats in the whole of London. Bye, bye, Jenny.'

'Bye, bye, Ben.'

Jenny picked up the letters from the counter where Ben had left them down as he was drinking his tea. She flicked through the mail. Brown bill, brown bill, brown bill, oh, white, she noticed. The postage stamp was from America. She didn't know anybody there. Her curiosity deepened. Just as she was about to open the big white envelope, the bell rang in the shop.

Two children approached the counter; their eyes open wide with astonishment at the sight of so many sweets.

'Our uncle is home from Australia,' they both shouted together. 'Look what he gave us!' Their fists were clenched tightly around the coins. Their uncle had divided the money equally between both of his nephews. They opened their fists and the money fell to the floor. The two children went onto their knees trying to recover the coins that rolled under the sweet boxes and under the counter.

'Come on,' said Jenny. 'We'll gather up all of your money and then you can tell me which chocolates you would like.'

'Thank you, thank you,' they cried. Soon, all the money was on the counter.

'I know, I know,' shouted the older of the boys. 'We'll buy one of the big boxes of chocolates, the one with the silky bow on it. They look yummy! We can share.'

'Yes,' replied his younger brother with assurance, 'Have you enough money there?'

'Plenty, boys,' said Jenny as she counted out the coins aloud. 'Guess what? You even have some change.'

'Thanks,' they shouted as they raced out through the door, their legs tipping their bottoms. 'Can't wait to try these. Let's put the change in our piggy banks.'

Jenny smiled to herself. The innocence of children! Without hesitation, she proceeded to open the letter from America. Her brow furrowed when she saw that there was another letter inside the envelope. How strange! The sealed envelope read: My darling daughter, Annie Jennifer Jones. Jenny began to feel faint. Oh, my God! George! I can't believe this! She went over to the shop door and locked it, turning the sign to closed. She didn't want any interruptions.

Jenny went into the kitchen, sat down at the table and laid the letter addressed to Annie in front of her. She started to read the letter addressed to her. As she read George's words, she felt a sense of numbness overcome her. After reading George's explanation and confession she felt utter disgust towards her once husband. Physically and emotionally, she was sickened. Such humiliation. 'A woman,' she said aloud. 'I will never accept this and I will never give him absolution, never!' What would the neighbours say? What would John Ellis think? More importantly, Annie must never be told about his dirty little secret.

She knew what she must do. No one would ever know. She snatched up the letter. 'Six pages,' she remarked aloud. 'Six pages of shame on all of the Jones and Crosby families. No more!' she cried, as she ran to the fireplace in the sitting room and set fire to the letter. 'Now,' she said, poking the ashes to make sure that nothing remained.

Jenny went back into the kitchen where she had left the letter addressed to Annie. After meditating for a while over the letter she decided to keep it because it was addressed to his daughter. She did not feel she had the right to burn or dispose of it. She decided to hide it in a drawer where she kept various family letters and stationery. She would lock this drawer and keep the key in her jewellery box for safety. She would have to act normally and never disclose to anyone what was uncovered on that horrible Monday morning.

Why couldn't he have died? she kept thinking. That would have been so much easier. Jenny was engulfed with total hatred for George, a feeling she had never felt before, for anybody or anything, in all of her lifetime. Life's a bitch, she said to herself.

CHAPTER 5

Emily and Grace invited Hope to their new house for the weekend. They were now well settled in their new home. They both missed their dearest friend very much. Hope jumped at the chance, after all, they were living in such a beautiful place with magnificent views all around – a mixture of green fields, trees, lakes and mountains - not to mention all that fresh air. What could be more tempting, given all that had been happening in her life at that time?

Hope packed her clothes, not forgetting her nice new leather hiking boots, which she had bought especially for this trip. She was finally ready for her three hour journey.

'I knew I forgot something,' she said aloud. 'Dynamite.' Hope rushed back inside to get her cat. 'Here puss, puss! Where are you? There you are, all tucked up in a little ball in your wicker basket, fast asleep. Forgive me, Dynamite. I almost went without you. Now, how could I leave you!' she exclaimed as she rubbed the cat's forehead with deep affection. 'Mustn't forget your cat food. You're such a good puss! Now puss, you can ride on the front seat with me and keep me company.'

'Meow! Meow!' purred Dynamite, as if in agreement with Hope's proposal. 'At last,' said Hope, putting on her safety belt, 'we're finally on our way.' She turned to Dynamite. 'I think we'll listen to some music on the journey. Do you like John Denver? Here goes,' she said as she slid the tape into the tape deck. Hope sang along and knew every word of every song but, unfortunately for Dynamite, she couldn't exactly reach those high notes quite like John Denver.

'Meow! Meow!' cried Dynamite and seemed to roll up more and more into a ball as if trying to block out Hope's singing.

'We're nearly there now, Dynamite, not long more. I think we'll pull over near this picnic area just ahead. I have some sandwiches and a flask of coffee. Don't worry,' she remarked to Dynamite. 'I have some tuna for you, your favourite.' Hope pulled the car over, opened the boot and took out her well-packed picnic basket. 'I think we'll eat in the car, it's a bit chilly outside.' She opened up her flask and poured herself a well-deserved cup of black coffee, just the way she liked it. 'Milk kills the real flavour of coffee,' she remarked. 'Just what I needed! Now, Dynamite, I haven't forgotten you.' Hope leaned over and fed Dynamite tuna from her own bowl. She placed the fish on the palm of her hand and, picking it up with her fingers, fed it directly into Dynamite's little mouth, which was watering with delight.

'Now,' said Hope as she wiped her mouth with her paper napkin and applied fresh lipstick, 'let us continue our journey, puss, my love.'

Grace and Emily had given Hope very clear directions and she had no problem finding the white house on a hilltop with the pink cherry blossom tree in the front garden. As soon as she arrived, Emily and Grace came running out to the car.

'Welcome, Hope and Dynamite. It's so great to see you both!'

'I have an apology to make, my dear Hope,' said Emily with a roguish smile.

'Oh no, what?' asked Hope, thinking something was wrong.

'Forgot to roll out the red carpet,' replied Emily.

'Ha, ha ha! Ah, but you did not lose that sense of humour,' remarked Hope with a grin. Grace rushed to carry Dynamite - still in her basket - into the house. Hope carried in her two cases and, of course, her hiking boots from the back seat.

Grace and Emily bombarded Hope with questions. 'Can't wait to catch up on the latest gossip. How's Mr. Roberts? How's everyone in the library?'

'Great,' replied Hope. 'They all send their love and best wishes to you both.'

'First of all, we'll put puss sleeping beside the range in the kitchen. She'll be warm and cosy there.'

'Great, lucky puss!' Hope said.

They gave Hope a personal tour, as they called it, of their new home. As they progressed from room to room,

Hope saw how proud Grace and Emily were of their beautiful new home and how happy they were in it. 'A house' Hope remarked, 'of great charm and warmth and a feeling of homeliness and peace. Priceless, my friends!' No matter which room you looked out of, every view was breathtaking. Emily and Grace had obviously done the right thing by moving there and retiring. 'A piece of heaven, that's that you have here,' Hope said to them.

'Well, thank you,' they both replied, 'what a lovely thing to say.'

'I hope your room is warm enough, Hope. We decided to leave the radiator on and we also have a spare hot water bottle,' Grace informed her. 'I'll put it in your bed later, before you retire.'

'You're spoiling me totally, both of you. I won't want to go home after all this pampering.'

'You must be hungry,' Emily volunteered. 'We have a roast in the oven. The potatoes and vegetables are cooking away as we speak.'

'The aroma is driving me crazy,' said Grace 'I can't wait to dig in.' The three ladies went into the kitchen to get the dinner organized.

'I'll set the table,' said Hope, 'and make myself useful.'

'I'll strain the potatoes and vegetables,' offered Emily.

'Well, there's nothing left for me then,' added Grace, 'but make the gravy.'

The three women continued with their tasks in the kitchen when, all of a sudden, they were interrupted by

Dynamite leaping out of her basket. She made her way across the kitchen floor hissing at something that was underneath the old cupboard. Out of nowhere, a gray, skinny mouse ran past, closely followed by Dynamite. 'Oh,' cried Emily in a wry tone. 'It looks like the mouse is in danger of being caught by Dynamite.' The others laughed at Emily's old familiar sharpness of wit. Soon, Dynamite came out from under the cupboard with the mouse in her mouth. She trotted across the kitchen floor and dropped the mouse at Hope's feet. She looked up at Hope as if to say: 'I prepared my own dinner!'

'Good puss!' said Emily, 'Grace and I have been trying to catch that mouse for ages.' Hope got a dustpan and brush and removed the dead mouse from the house. She threw it outside among old briars and bushes and then she went back into the kitchen, washed her hands and sat down with Emily and Grace at the table. After dinner, they all helped with clearing the dinner table and washing up.

'Many hands make light work, I always say,' said Grace.

By the time they had finished, darkness was setting in. 'I'll close the curtains and we'll all have a night-cap,' said Grace. 'Let's go into the lounge and sit beside the open log fire.'

'That sounds great,' Hope said rubbing her hands together. 'I brought two bottles of Bourbon. I have them upstairs in my bag. A little house-warming present. I know you both like a little drop of Bourbon on very special occasions and this is certainly a very special occasion.'

'We won't refuse!' piped up both women simultaneously. They all laughed. The three women chatted and chatted for hours.

'I'm feeling a bit tipsy,' remarked Hope.

'No wonder you do,' replied Emily. 'I'm not counting your glasses, but believe it or not girls, we drank one full bottle.' Hope certainly was drinking Emily and Grace under the proverbial table.

'I've definitely had enough alcohol,' said Grace, emitting a stream of hiccups. 'Oh, sorry!' she giggled, with yet another hiccup.

'I want to make a toast,' said Hope. 'To my dearest, most beautiful friends.' She raised her glass with a struggle and tried not to stagger too much. 'There is so much, my friends, that you don't know about me.' Grace and Emily interrupted gently.

'You have had more than too much to drink, dear Hope. You should go and sleep it off.'

'No, no,' replied Hope, 'I'm not finished. There's so much you deserve to know about me. I want to tell you. Please, please, listen to me.' Hope's voice was slurred but commanded authority at the same time.

'Ok,' said Emily 'We're listening to what you have to say.' Emily and Grace sat into the couch, listening attentively to what Hope wanted to tell them.

'I, my friends, was born a man,' Hope shouted out. My name was G-G-G-George. I was married and I have a beautiful daughter. They live in London.' Tears flowed down Hope's face. The glass from which she was drinking slipped from her fingers and fell with a crash onto the wooden floor. She fell to her knees. 'Sorry. I am so, so sorry,' Hope apologized as she went to pick up the pieces of glass, cutting her fingers instead.

Both Emily and Grace ran to her rescue and lifted her up onto the couch, placing two plump, lavender coloured cushions behind her head. Grace ran to the first-aid box and got a plaster and disinfectant for the wounds on her fingers. Emily and Grace looked at one another. Both sets of eyes filled with tears and pain for what they had just heard from poor, beautiful Hope.

'First things first,' said Grace. 'Let's get you cleaned up. We'll talk about this in the morning. You're in no fit state to talk tonight.' As soon as Grace had spoken these words, Hope collapsed into a deep sleep. Emily and Grace fluffed up the cushions under her head and put a warm patchwork quilt over her. They kissed Hope on the forehead, switched off the light, agreeing that she'd be fine there on the couch until the morning.

Hope was awakened by an unusual sensation on her forehead. 'What the? Oh, it's you, Dynamite.' The cat licked her forehead with affection. 'Come on,' she said, as she stretched and remembered what had been said the night before. 'Let's get you a bowl of milk, puss.' Hope, feeling very much the worse for ware, dragged herself out to the kitchen and went to the fridge to get Dynamite her bowl of milk. She had a thumping headache so she sat down at the kitchen table holding her head with both hands. Bit by bit, the events of the night before came back to her. She hoped she hadn't frightened Emily and Grace off with her disclosure. They probably wouldn't want anything more to do with her now. She didn't know how she was going to face them, she felt so embarrassed. It was only just eight a.m. and she considered leaving before they got up.

'Good morning!' The kitchen door swung open and Emily and Grace both appeared in their dressing gowns and slippers.

'Good morning,' replied Hope, not knowing what was going to happen or to be said next.

'Now, Hope, we both had a discussion upstairs earlier in regard to what you have told us about your life,' said Emily.

'But, but,' interrupted Hope.

'Please, just listen to what we have to say and please don't interrupt until we have said our piece, ok?'

'Ok,' replied Hope, her head bowed.

'Before we have this conversation,' said Grace, 'I think we should all have some bacon and eggs, toast and a pot of very strong coffee. We may be feeling a little bit delicate, but it would help soak up all that alcohol. Then we'll talk.'

'As I said earlier,' Emily pulled her chair closer to Hope as she spoke, 'just listen. No interruptions.' She reached out and held Hope's trembling hands. 'First of all, you are our friend. We love you dearly. We can't even imagine the pain and hurt you are going through. We want to help you through your pain and sadness. You're a wonderful person and, most of all, a child of God with such wonderful qualities.'

'I never had a family,' remarked Grace, 'but I know one thing for sure. If I did have a family and you were my child, boy or girl, I would be so proud of you. What you have gone through!'

'That is the nicest thing anyone has ever said to me,' Hope said, fighting back the tears.

'The same goes for me,' Emily added. 'God love you, you must feel so alone. Would you mind sharing the full story of your life with your two best friends? We want to know everything so that we can help you in every way we can. Sometimes Hope, it's better to share your pain, rather than carry your cross all alone. We will never let you down and that's a promise. Now, I know I'm not as fast on the feet as I used to be but it's a lovely sunny day, so why don't we go for a nice walk and put some colour back into our cheeks.'

'Come on girls,' said Grace, let's fight this together. After all, they say there's strength in numbers.'

'Can I speak now?' asked Hope.

'Yes,' replied Emily and Grace together, as if rehearsed.

'I can't begin to tell you how much you both mean to me. You have restored my faith in mankind and given me back a sense of self worth. God bless you both, from the bottom of my heart. I read somewhere that the majority of people are under the illusion that we human beings can only meet with one soul mate in our lifetime. I am so lucky because I have, in fact, found two.' All three hugged one another tightly, overwhelmed with emotion and affection.

Emily and Grace slipped into their ankle socks and comfortable walking shoes for their walk. 'I don't know where you think you're going, Hope, with those hiking boots. Wait until you get to my age and you suffer with corns and bunions,' said Grace, looking skeptically at Hope's new hiking boots. Hope knew how hard Emily and Grace were trying to make light of her hard, difficult situation as they walked. She felt herself slowly releasing to her two, dear friends, the story of her troubled life.

The three women walked for miles and miles on that beautiful sunny afternoon. Grace and Emily listened very attentively to every word that Hope uttered. Hope could see many different expressions appear on their faces as they both struggled emotionally with what they were hearing. Of all those emotions that Hope could read so clearly, sadness and shock were the two most repeated expressions. To listen to someone speaking – really, really listen to what they say is so important and is a gift that not many people possess. Both Emily and Grace had that precious gift. They listened but never commented or judged while Hope let them into her world of hidden secrets.

Hope was interrupted by the sound of the church bells ringing. They were announcing the commencement of the six o'clock Mass, celebrated daily by Father Patrick Mulcahy, an Irish priest for whom Emily and Grace had a special fondness. Every Sunday, without fail, they would cook Sunday lunch for Father Mulcahy - Irish stew - his favourite. He had brought the recipe from Ireland and given it to Emily. He always looked forward to Sundays, not just for the delicious lunch, but also his glass of Sherry, which they nicknamed a little 'tosheen' – an Irish saying, no doubt!

Hope had said all there was to say. Now, Emily and Grace felt it was time to make a plan and, hopefully, bring some happiness back into Hope's life. But how? How could this be achieved?

Later that evening, the three ladies tucked into a very late supper of fried potatoes and some cold chicken and salad that were leftovers from lunch. Afterwards, they decided to retire to the living room, put up their aching feet and snuggle up nice and cosy in front of the log fire. 'Anyone for drinks, girls?' asked Emily.

'No, not for me,' replied Grace, 'I'll never let a drop of alcohol pass my lips again. No more hangovers for me. I'll just have a nice mug of cocoa,' she laughed.

'That sounds so tempting,' said Hope. 'That's exactly what I would like too.' She jumped up from her armchair. 'I'll make it. Three cups of steaming hot cocoa coming up!'

'You know what, ladies?' said Grace. 'I've come up with a plan.'

'Oh yeah?' said Hope and Emily at the same time.

'Hope, I think you should go back to London and take

the bull by the horns and meet your long-lost daughter. That, in my opinion, is the only thing to do. Then you should go back and visit your parents and family in Wales, but I have to say your daughter should be your first priority. You have to at least try.'

'All the times I dreamed of meeting my daughter and loved ones again,' responded Hope.

'I agree one hundred per cent with Grace,' said Emily. 'You have to go back and at least try. Time goes by so quickly, you don't want another ten years to slip by.'

'No doubt about it,' Grace offered, 'life's a bitch but we all have to fight back, especially when we are hardest hit. As a frog croaks, a glow-worm glows and each is perfect amongst its own, so too, it is with you, Hope. Please remember these words.

With the support of Emily and Grace, Hope felt stronger now than she had felt in a long time. 'It's a couple of months since I wrote to Jenny. I had given up on getting a reply. She obviously reacted the way I feared she would. I think I'll have to go back in person. I have two weeks' vacation due at the end of the month. That gives me three weeks to get organized.'

Emily and Grace offered to help Hope financially with the flight and hotel expenses. They would not take no for an answer. Hope agreed to accept their kind offer. After all, in her eyes, they were family.

Sunday morning arrived, the day of Hope's departure.

The sound of Grace singing cheerfully and the aroma of freshly made pancakes escaping from the kitchen awakened her. 'Get up, Hope, and come down here for breakfast.' Hope jumped out of bed and put on her dressing gown and slippers, deciding to leave her bath until after breakfast. When Grace, Hope and Emily sat at the kitchen table that Sunday morning, the same thought crossed each of their minds: this might be the last time they would all be together. Hope might decide to stay in London to become reacquainted with her daughter. It was the only time that not one of them shared what they were thinking. It was as if none of them really wanted to face what lay ahead in the coming weeks.

Hope and Dynamite were all packed and ready for their journey home. Emily and Grace hugged Hope, wishing her the best of luck. 'Now, Hope,' said Emily, 'if, for some reason, things don't work out for you in London, we want you to know that you are welcome to come and live with us. It would be our privilege to have you but we're certain that your daughter will accept you and will want you back in her life. Be positive, Hope, dreams can come true.'

'Now, my friend, we have a little good luck charm for you,' said Grace, handing her a red velvet box.

'Oh!' cried Hope, choked with emotion, as she took from the box a beautiful silver chain and medal of St. Anthony. Emily and Grace knew of her devotion to this gentlest of all saints. 'Thank you both so much. I'll treasure it and wear it always,' she said, as Grace helped her tie the clasp around her neck.

'Now, here's a few dollars to help you on your way,' said Emily, handing Hope a brown envelope.

'I don't know how I can ever repay either of you,' Hope said as she fought back the tears.

'There is one way you can. Go win back your daughter. We want so much to meet her.'

CHAPTER 6

Unconditional Love

Written for you, my dearest daughter, with all my love.

I would climb the highest mountain,
Swim the deepest sea,
Fight the largest army,
For you to be with me.
I would walk across a desert,
I would gladly brave the storm,
Knowing at the end of it,
I was there to keep you warm.

You do not feel the same my love,
So I have to let you go.
My love is like an acorn,
Ready to grow and grow.
Remember how much I love you,
Remember how much you meant,
Most of all remember,
To me you were heaven sent.

Hope was reading from her book of poems. Poetry had always been dear to her heart and she found that writing her own poems was a good way of expressing her feelings. There were two poems in particular that she had written with her daughter, Annie Jennifer Jones, in mind. She hardly dared hope that she might somehow get a chance to read them out to her but she sat down at her writing table and transcribed these two to take with her to London, just in case.

Hope remembered fondly the time she had told her small daughter that she had a guardian angel and that everybody had one because we all need to be loved and minded by God's angels. She smiled now as she wrote out the second poem, remembering how comforted Annie had felt by the thought of these invisible friends and how it had prompted Hope to write this poem for her daughter.

Our Guardian Angels

We all have a guardian angel, given from God above,
Trained up in the Heavens, filled with the ingredient love.
There's an angel for every baby, in every walk of life,
Day by day, night my night, to help us thorough our strife.

Sometimes they try and tell us when danger is very near,
That's how we get a feeling of overwhelming fear.
So listen very attentively for what they have to say,
They are trying to bring you safely, through another day.

We are so very special, that we cannot hide,
Given a friend of Jesus, in whom we can confide.
Always there beside you, helping you to grow,
So say a little thank you, for your love to show.

You can always hide beneath their wings,
When trouble comes your way.
They'll fight for you and help you through,
Another lonely day.

Hope took out some photographs of dear Granny Annie Jenny as well as that sweet photograph of Baby Annie Jennifer Jones, born 4 September. She placed these in her handbag. She also carried this photograph of Annie in a gold locket around her neck, her child's name and date of birth engraved on the locket and in her heart. The other precious memory she wore around her neck was the St. Anthony medal given to her by the friends she now called her family.

The next thing she needed to sort out was her wardrobe. Emily and Grace always consulted Hope when shopping for clothes because she had such a great dress sense. In addition to her casual clothing, she decided she would bring her navy blue pencil shaped skirt with the nice shaped three quarter length jacket, navy bag and those navy court shoes for comfort. She would also pack her black skirt and the white Victorian style blouse with the black ribbon around the cuffs. Her black button earrings and navy drop earrings would complement these outfits. She decided to wear her black shoulder length hair tied up in a bun at the back. This is who I am now, she thought. Hope held the holy medal, asking St. Anthony once again to help her through all that lay ahead. 'Give me strength now,' she said aloud, struggling with her bulging suitcase on the bed. She had to kneel on it to close the zip. At last it was closed. She gave a sigh of relief. The only thing left for her to do now was to see to Dynamite.

Hope's next-door neighbour, Michael, a seventy-year-old retired plumber, had a great love of animals. He helped out all the neighbours, never refusing to look after their pets in any given crisis or when they went on vacation. He liked to feel that he was still needed. 'She'll be company for me,' he said to Hope when she brought Dynamite over to him.

'I have food for Dynamite here in the bag,' Hope said, putting it down on the floor near the fridge.

'That's great,' said Michael. 'Now, don't you worry about a thing. Enjoy your vacation and have a safe journey.'

'Thanks very much, Michael. I'll bring you back a present,' Hope remarked as she walked out the door.

'Just bring yourself back,' shouted Michael. 'That's all we want'.

'Bye, bye, Michael.'

'Goodbye Hope! See you in a week.'

Hope's taxi arrived and the taxi driver helped her with her bags. 'How long are you going for?' he asked.

'Just a week,' replied Hope.

'Sure don't seem like you're going for a week, feels more like a month. What a weight!' he laughed heartily.

'That's women for you,' replied Hope with a grin. 'Everything but the kitchen sink!'

At last, Hope was in the plane, ready for her long flight to London. It had been a long day and she decided to take a sleeping tablet so that she would be able to get some rest. Seated in front of her were a mother and daughter. Hope couldn't but envy the closeness they showed towards one another. She wondered if she would ever share that experience with her own daughter. Some day, please God, some day.

CHAPTER 7

The small hotel that Hope had booked into was only about twenty minutes' drive from Crosby's sweet shop. She was familiar with it from the time she had lived in London and worked in the bakery because there was a daily order of bread and cakes from the London Leisure Hotel.

'Looks like rain,' said the taxi driver. 'I don't like the look of that sky.' No sooner had he spoken the words than the sky started to open, sending down sheets of rain.

'How much do I owe you?' asked Hope, rooting around her bag for her purse.

'Five pounds for you, Miss,' said the taxi driver. 'We'll have to make a run for it or we'll be like drowned rats in this downpour. I'll get your luggage.'

'Thanks,' replied Hope, as she swung the door open. 'Oops! Typical, I've stepped in a pool of water.' She had just decided to put her coat over her head to protect her shiny black hair from getting wet when the hotel porter ran over with a large umbrella emblazoned with the black and yellow crest of the London Leisure Hotel.

Hope had time to look around her, as both receptionists were busy with other guests. She noticed that very little had changed in the ten years she was away. The chandeliers and quaint furniture were the same. The walls had been newly decorated in a cream and gold wallpaper, while rich red pile carpet covered the floors. On the walls hung a collection of black and white photographs of old buildings. She walked over to them and viewed them with interest. And there it was, the familiar narrow cobblestone street of St. James' Lane. There was the bridal shop, the old bakery where she had once worked and the shop that now housed her dreams, Crosby's Handmade Chocolates. Hope felt her throat tighten.

After unpacking, Hope decided to have a nice hot bath. That was one thing she loved about staying in hotels, there was always plenty of hot water. After her bath, she dressed for dinner and went down to the hotel restaurant for dinner. She browsed through the menu. 'I think I'll have the crispy duck with vegetables and potatoes and an extra serving of orange sauce,' she said to the waiter.

'Certainly, Madam,' he replied. 'Would Madam like to see the wine list?'

'That won't be necessary. A glass of your house wine will do just fine. Red, please,' Hope said with a smile, laying her napkin neatly on her lap.

'As you wish, Madam.'

In the dining room that evening, Hope noticed that she was the only one dining alone. It seemed that each table told a different story. One couple held hands while gazing lovingly into each other's eyes. Another table had a party of four, two young couples who toasted aloud the announcement of their engagements and were also planning a double wedding in six months' time. As Hope looked at the burning candle that flickered on her table, she said a silent prayer. Please God; grant me a bit of happiness.

'One crispy duck for you, Madam, not forgetting Madam's extra helping of orange sauce. Bon appetit.'

'Thank you, that looks lovely,' said Hope with a smile.

The laughter, the love and outpouring of emotion from the different couples seemed to make Hope more aware of her own problems and loneliness. She was happy to see other people enjoying life but one question kept echoing in her mind and heart: what is life if you haven't got anyone to share it with?

'Is everything to your satisfaction, Madam? Would you like to order dessert?' Hope, distracted by her thoughts, didn't hear the waiter. He repeated his words.

'Oh, sorry, what did you say? No, thank you,' she said, getting up from the table. 'I am retiring. I have had a long day. The meal was delicious. Good night.'

Before leaving the dining room, Hope approached the young couples' table.

'Excuse me. I couldn't help but overhear your engagement and wedding plans. I just want to say that I wish all four of you much joy and happiness', she said in a caring and sincere manner. 'Life is for living. To find someone you love is one of life's finest blessings'.

'Why thank you, that's so kind of you', replied one of the women with a gracious smile. The others nodded their heads in agreement, smiling and thanking Hope at the same time.

'Good luck and good wishes to you', said Hope, as she walked away.

Tired as she was, Hope tossed and turned for hours that night, rehearsing over and over again the words she would say to the mother of her child, the woman who, undoubtedly, held the key to her future. She found it hard to believe that so many years had passed and now, all of a sudden, she was only hours away from meeting all her past blessings and demons. At two a.m. she finally got up to get a sleeping pill. Tomorrow of all days, she wanted to look her best. Slowly, she drifted off to sleep.

Hope awoke to a tap on the door. It was room service with the breakfast she had ordered. 'Good morning', said the young girl entering her room with a bright smile. 'Full English, Miss. I wish I could eat like that but I only have to look at food and I seem to put on weight. Look at you, you're as slim as a pencil,' she laughed guilelessly.

'You look perfect to me,' said Hope to the girl. 'In all sincerity, I guess none of us are really ever happy with ourselves.'

'You're probably right', said the girl. 'I had better continue on by breakfast round or I'll be in trouble. Good morning, Miss.'

'Have a nice day,' replied Hope. A nice day, thought Hope to herself. I am terrified this is going to be the best or worst day of my life. She settled down to eat her breakfast but abandoned the idea. She just couldn't face food this morning. She decided to have a bath instead. Hope spent one full hour getting ready until, at last, she was happy with how she looked. 'Now for the final and most important touch', she said aloud. She sat on the edge of the bed and tied her most treasured possessions around her neck: her locket with the picture and date of birth of her daughter and her St Anthony medal, engraved with love from her dearest friends, Emily and Grace. These two treasured items were also her good luck charms. God, did she need them today.

'Now,' she said aloud, 'what else do I need?' She rooted around her bag for the two poems she had written for her daughter. She sealed them in an envelope, which she addressed to Miss Annie Jennifer Jones, St. James' Lane, London. Not for the first time, she hoped she would get a chance to read them to her personally.

'Money? Yes,' she checked her purse. She had everything. The clasp of her handbag snapped loudly as she closed it. She called reception to order a taxi.

For the next half hour or so, Hope paced up and down her room nervously until the receptionist rang to let her know her taxi had arrived. She hurried downstairs.

'Good morning, what's your destination, Miss?' said her taxi driver, looking at Hope in his rear mirror.

St. James' Lane,' she replied, her voice shaking.

'Have you there in a jiffy.'

As they neared the street, Hope found herself feeling faint with fear.

'I can get out here. I need to stretch my legs.'

'No problem, Miss. That'll be three pounds, please.'

Hope paid the taxi driver and stepped out onto the old cobble stone street. She stood underneath the lamppost where she had often stood all those years ago. She could see clearly that quaint old shop, Crosby's Handmade Chocolates. There it was at last, that timeless little shop that was once her home. She stood there for some time, watching people going in and out of it.

It's time, she thought, I have to face this. She walked slowly across the street, entering the shop to the familiar clang of that same old bell. 'Be with you in a second', shouted a voice from the back kitchen. Hope watched with awe as Jenny approached the counter. Despite the passing of time, despite all she had gone through, Jenny was as beautiful as ever. A timeless, unspoilt beauty, Hope thought, and felt comforted.

'Hello, how can I help you, Madam?' Jennifer Jones asked politely.

'I'd like a box of your handmade truffles,' replied Hope.

'You have good taste,' said Jennifer with a smile, handing Hope her box of chocolate truffles. At that moment, Hope caught her hand firmly.

'It's me, Jennifer, don't be frightened.'

'What? Who? Oh my God, it's you. It is you! What have you done? Get out! Get out!' Jenny shouted as she rushed to open the door.

'I need to talk to you, please! Please! Jenny don't turn me away!' Hope pleaded.

'What have you done to yourself? Look at you, a man wearing a skirt! You're a freak! A freak! I can't bear to look at you; you disgust me!' Jenny shouted, pushing Hope towards the open door. 'Get out! Get out of my life! Crawl back to wherever you have been for the last ten years. If you have any decency or any love for your daughter, you will listen to me. Go and do not ever, ever come back!'

Jenny pushed Hope out onto the street and locked the door behind her.

CHAPTER 8

Utterly distraught and broken, Hope walked the streets for miles in a daze. She had no goal, no destination. She walked for hours.

Eventually, she realised she had come to the same woods where she and Jenny used to come for walks. She walked on until she came to a field. There was the old hay barn in which they had often sheltered from the rain. Hope walked into the barn and stood there, looking around. She saw the bales of hay in front of her and smelled their tangy freshness. She noticed the neat arrangement of farm implements up against the left wall. To her right was a smallish horsebox, used to transport cattle and hay.

Hope looked up at the rafters of the shed. She saw a rope hanging down from one of the beams. She reached up and pulled it down, bringing with it a cloud of dust. A million thoughts raced through her mind. She thought of all the uses this old rope had had. She imagined the farmer using it to tie up the gate; to help when cows were calving; to tie down the hay. He possibly even used this rope to tie his old Comby coat when the buttons went missing in the cold winter months.

The old rope had one final use. This rope could take all her pain away. It could take away the pain she was inflicting on others. She remembered something her grandmother had said to her many years ago. *A bird can sing with a broken wing but not with a broken heart.* No words had ever made as much sense to her in all her life. Those words said it all.

Hope clasped her locket and holy medal tightly. Tears flowed down her face as she said her final act of contrition. Forgive me, Father.

Hush! Hush! Now, George, know how much I love you. Yes, until the end of time. You are precious; you are my child. You have carried your cross just like me. Rest now. I shall give you peace.

Hope's lifeless body hanged from the old rope, heavy, but now unburdened. A small bird that had always sung so sweetly swept down and perched lovingly on her head. That bird sang no more.

A bird can sing

with a broken wing -

but not with

a broken heart . . .